CHOOSE YOUR OW

Kids Love Reading
Choose Your Own Adventure®!

"It's like a new book every time I pick it up."
Quin Carpenter, age 9

"I love all the riddles they are so fun! I can't wait to finish it at home, I did not know there were so many ways to go!"
Charlotte Young, age 9

"You never know what's going to happen next!"
Skylar Stoudt, age 8

"I like how it was me choosing what to do and how it felt to actually be the main character."
Wilson Stack, age 9

"These books are the best!
They make it so you're the character."
Josslyn Jewett, age 9

Your Baby Unicorn © 2021 Chooseco LLC,
Waitsfield, Vermont. All Rights Reserved.

Illustrated by Darren McKee
Book design by Stacey Boyd, Big Eyedea Visual Design
For information regarding permission, write to:

CHOOSECO
P.O. Box 46, Waitsfield, Vermont 05673
www.cyoa.com

A DRAGONLARK BOOK

Names: Falligant, Erin, author. | McKee, Darren, illustrator.
Title: Your baby unicorn / by Erin Falligant ; illustrated by Darren McKee.
Other Titles: Choose your own adventure. Dragonlarks.
Description: Waitsfield, Vermont : Chooseco, [2021] | Interest age level: 005-008. | Summary: "When your new baby brother arrives, your parents understand that you're a little jealous. They give you something of your very own to care for—a pony named Sunny. But you soon discover a secret about Sunny: she's not a pony at all. Sunny is a baby unicorn! Can you keep it a secret?"--Provided by publisher.
Identifiers: ISBN 9781937133795 | ISBN 1937133796
Subjects: LCSH: Unicorns--Juvenile fiction. | Animals--Infancy--Juvenile fiction. | Brothers and sisters--Juvenile fiction. | Secrecy--Juvenile fiction. | CYAC: Unicorns--Fiction. | Brothers and sisters--Fiction. | Secrecy--Fiction. | Animals--Infancy--Fiction. | LCGFT: Fantasy fiction. | Choose-your-own stories.
Classification: LCC PZ7.F1959 Re 2021 | DDC [E]--dc23

Published simultaneously in the United States and Canada

Printed in China

11 10 9 8 7 6 5 4 3 2

CHOOSE YOUR OWN ADVENTURE®

Your Baby Unicorn

BY ERIN FALLIGANT

ILLUSTRATED BY DARREN MCKEE

A DRAGONLARK BOOK

For Maya, lover of unicorns.

READ THIS FIRST!!!

WATCH OUT!
THIS BOOK IS DIFFERENT
from every book you've ever read.

Do not read this book from the first page
through to the last page.
Instead, start on page 1 and read until you
come to your first choice. Then turn to the
page shown and see what happens.

When you come to the end of a story,
you can go back and start again.
Every choice leads to a new adventure.

Good luck!

You grab some carrots and race through the kitchen. Your baby brother, Jack, waves from his high chair.

Dad wipes his hands on his apron. "Carrots for breakfast? Wouldn't a muffin be tastier?" he asks you, wiggling his eyebrows.

"The carrots are for Sunny," you explain. Sunny, your new pony, is waiting for you in the stable!

Turn to the next page.

2

As you push open the door, you spot your best friend, Grace, walking her dog, Waffles. Grace spins in a circle to untangle herself from the leash. "Will you ride your new pony over later?" she calls to you.

"Yes!" you say. "I can't wait!"

Turn to page 4.

4

Sunny whinnies from inside the stable. She's very small, with soft gray hair. She's a baby, just like your brother, Jack. When she sees you, she starts to shimmer. Her gray coat glows. *Pop!* Something suddenly sprouts between her ears.

You step backward. "Is that a . . . horn?" you whisper.

"Why, yes!"

You hear the words clearly. But who said them? As Sunny munches on the carrots you brought, she stares at you with bright eyes.

"Can you talk, Sunny?" you ask.

"Of course!" She leans forward, as if she's been waiting forever to talk to you.

Your jaw drops. Not only do you have your own baby unicorn—she talks!

Turn to page 6.

Sunny paces in her stall. "Can I come out now?" she begs.

You hesitate. "What if my parents don't let me keep a unicorn?"

"Oh," says Sunny. "Right." As she lowers her head, her horn vanishes with a *poof*, and she fades to pale gray.

"Don't worry!" you say, giving her a pat. "Let me think."

Go on to the next page.

Your stay-at-home dad goes with the flow, but your mom likes to know what's coming next. She develops software that predicts the weather, and she's not into magical things like unicorns.

I can't tell my parents, you decide. But could you tell your best friend, Grace?

If you keep your unicorn a secret, turn to the next page.

If you choose to tell Grace, turn to page 12.

8

Just as you decide to keep your unicorn a secret, Dad brings a plate of muffins out to the stable.

"Blueberry Crumb Cruffins," he announces. "My winning recipe for the Berry Days Festival this weekend."

As he sets down the plate, Sunny's nostrils quiver. Then her coat starts to shimmer. *Uh-oh,* you think.

You rush Dad out of the stable. "I smell something burning," you say. "Better check the oven!"

The second Dad leaves, Sunny goes full-on unicorn. She gobbles a muffin off the plate and reaches for another.

"No more muffins!" you say. "Ponies eat oats."

"Oh, drat," says Sunny. Her horn *poofs* away.

Turn to page 10.

You give Sunny a scoop of oats.

"No, thanks," she says with a sniff. But when a dog barks, she pricks up her ears. *Pop!* sprouts her horn.

Through the window, you see the neighbor boys chasing their yappy Yorkie in circles.

"Can I play too?" Sunny begs.

Go on to the next page.

"They'll see your horn!" you whisper.

"Please?" says Sunny. She paws at the ground, accidentally knocking over the pail of oats. *Crash!*

The pail, which now rests upside down like a hat, gives you an idea. Could you cover up Sunny's horn with a hat? Or should you calm her down with the treat she really wants—another muffin?

If you want to find a hat for Sunny, turn to page 16.

If you choose to give Sunny a muffin, turn to page 22.

12

Dad says you can go see Grace, but only if you take your little brother. So you, Jack, and Sunny set off toward Grace's house. Grace is dancing across the yard, and her big brother, Mason, is teaching their dog how to roll over.

At the sight of Waffles, the goldendoodle, Sunny starts to shimmer.

"Uh-oh," she whispers. Only you hear.

"What a cute pony!" calls Grace.

Mason glances up. "I'll bet your pony can't do this." When he snaps his fingers, Waffles rolls over. "We're going to win the dog show at the Berry Days Festival this weekend."

Then he tosses his baseball, and Waffles leaps to catch it. Sunny leaps, too. *Pop!* sprouts her horn.

"Whoa!" says Grace. A coil of hair springs loose from her ponytail.

Turn to page 15.

Mason's eyes widen. "That horn isn't real. No way." He tugs on it.

"Ouch!" says Sunny, tugging back.

Grace sucks in her breath. "She talks, too?"

"Don't tell anyone!" you cry.

"Why not?" says Mason. "If I had a talking unicorn, I'd tell *everyone*. I'd show her off at Berry Days! Hey, we should do a dog-and-pony act after the parade. We'd win for sure!"

He rubs his hands together as if he can't wait to get them on that blue ribbon. Grace's eyes flash. You know she wants you to say yes, too.

*If you agree to the act,
turn to page 24.*

*If you say no,
turn to page 40.*

16

Just as you find a witch's hat in your costume box, Dad asks if you'll watch your brother. Jack pulls fairy wings and a lion's mane out of the box. You dress him in the costume and carry your Lion Fairy brother out to the stable.

When Sunny sees Jack, she pops her horn. She shimmers even brighter when you place the hat on her head. "A dress-up party?" she says. "Yes, please!"

"It's just a disguise," you explain. "So we can take you outside!" You lead her out of the stable.

When the boys next door see you, they scurry down from their treehouse. Their Yorkie yaps, and Sunny shimmers. You hold your breath, hoping her hat will stay on.

Turn to page 18.

18

"Hey, it's not Halloween!" says Brayden, the older brother.

You shrug. "Any day can be dress-up day."

"But we're not dressed up!" says little Ben. He rubs his *eye*, streaking dirt across his cheek.

Go on to the next page.

"Not *yet*," says Brayden. He waves Ben into the house. When they come out, Brayden is a superhero and Ben is a dinosaur with untied shoes.

"Costume parade!" declares Brayden. He marches behind Sunny. You lead the "parade" around the yard, until the boys' mom stops you.

"I'm organizing the Berry Days parade," says Mrs. Zimmerman. "Do you and your pony want to be in it?"

"Yes, please!" Sunny says. But Mrs. Zimmerman thinks *you* said it.

"Great!" she says. "Meet me at the fairgrounds tomorrow at nine o'clock."

Turn to the next page.

You're worried about parading your unicorn in front of the whole town. But when your parents say you can *ride* Sunny in the parade, you're thrilled!

You ride Sunny proudly past the crowd. Your dad holds Jack, in his costume, who waves and cheers. The neighbor boys walk alongside. "Happy Berry Days!" Brayden the superhero shouts into his megaphone. Ben the dinosaur chases a butterfly.

When you reach a street corner, a kid cheers and waves his corn dog. Sunny freezes.

"Oh, no," Sunny says, her eyes wide. "Not a corn dog." She starts to shake.

You just discovered one kind of dog Sunny *doesn't* like!

As Sunny steps backward, she trips over a Berry Days banner. You hear the *beep* of a clown car and the crash of a tuba.

If you tell Sunny to go past the corn dog, turn to page 26.

If you let Sunny turn around, turn to page 44.

You give Sunny another muffin. It makes her so happy, she's practically floating out of her stall. "Let's go for a ride!" she says. "An adventure, just you and me!"

Go on to the next page.

You're not sure what Sunny means by "adventure," but you'd love to find out! "Maybe we can ride in the woods out back," you say. "Where no one will see us."

"Yes!" Sunny shines so bright, you almost have to cover your eyes.

You check to make sure the neighbor boys have gone back in. Then you hear a car engine. Mom must be home! Do you ride Sunny out to the woods quickly, or do you ask Mom first?

*If you ask Mom first,
turn to page 28.*

*If you choose to ride Sunny without asking,
turn to page 36.*

You, Grace, and Mason put together a pretty cool dog-and-pony act.

It goes like this: Mason throws the baseball, Waffles leaps to catch it, and Sunny leaps after her. Waffles brings the ball to Jack for a treat, and Jack rolls the ball back to Mason. You even get to ride Sunny for part of the act, with Grace kneeling behind you.

Go on to the next page.

Now you can't wait to show everyone what Sunny can do! But your parents don't know about your unicorn yet. Should you reveal her secret during the act? Or tell your parents first?

*If you decide to wait until the act,
turn to page 48.*

*If you'd like to tell your parents first,
turn to page 56.*

"Sunny, let's go!" you say, tapping her sides with your feet.

She finally bolts past the corn dog. When the crowd ahead sees her, they cheer. Sunny puffs up with pride. As she prances and tosses her head, the witch hat topples off her horn.

"Oops!" she says.

"Hey!" Brayden shouts into his megaphone. "It's a unicorn!"

Everyone stares at you and Sunny. You think fast and search the crowd for your dad and brother. "Jack, can I borrow your fairy wings?" You attach the wings to Sunny's saddle and say to the crowd, "It's just another costume. See? She's a flying unicorn."

Brayden grins. "Happy Berry Days!" he says. "From the flying unicorn!"

Phew! Everyone cheers at Sunny's costume. Only you, Jack, and Sunny know she's not wearing one!

The End

Mom says you can ride Sunny, but she wants to help you saddle her up. She comes into the stable before you can stop her.

"Hello!" says Sunny, your shimmering unicorn. Mom steps backward and knocks over a rake. "Um, I n-need to talk to your father about this," she stammers. As she rushes out the door, your stomach sinks.

Turn to the next page.

"Sorry," says Sunny, lowering her head. "So sorry."

When Mom comes back, she's made a decision. "We signed up for a pony," she reminds you. "But this is an unusual pony. I think she'll be happier back at the farm where we got her."

How can you convince Mom to let you keep Sunny?

You think fast.

"Jack will be so sad!" you blurt out. "He wanted to ride Sunny."

Mom's face softens. "You can give him a ride after dark, when the neighbors won't see that she's a unicorn."

That night, you help Jack into Sunny's saddle. When you climb on too, Sunny is so happy, she prances.

"Oh, my," Sunny says. "This'll be fun!"

As you trot around the yard, you can almost feel Sunny's hooves leaving the ground. Wait, her hooves *are* leaving the ground. You soar past the neighbors' treehouse. You're flying!

Turn to page 32.

"Sunny, be careful!" you cry, hanging on to Jack. But as you soar over your house, your heart soars too. With the wind in your face and the streetlights below, this feels like a dream.

Sunny flies high above the neighborhood. If someone looked up, you're pretty sure they'd think they saw a shooting star.

"Moon!" cries Jack, reaching for the glowing moon.

Sunny floats higher.

"Whoa!" you say with a laugh. "We can't go to the moon today. We should get home before Mom misses us. She doesn't want a unicorn. She for sure doesn't want a *flying* unicorn."

Turn to page 34.

You land in the yard just as Mom comes back outside.

"Moon!" Jack cries. "More!" He raises his hands for another ride.

Mom sighs. "He really does like to ride," she says. "Maybe we could keep Sunny at a boarding stable, where you and Jack could take riding lessons."

Yes! you think. You hug Jack. Sometimes having a baby brother is a pain, but Jack came through for you today.

Then you hug Sunny, who glows with happiness. You can't wait to take her for another flight—er, ride. Where will you go next?

The End

36

You saddle up Sunny as quickly as you can. You can hardly wait to ride your unicorn!

Sunny seems excited, too. She canters toward the woods.

"Woo-hoo!" you holler, watching the ground fly past.

"Yes!" she says. "Isn't this wonderful?"

When you reach the woods, you suck in your breath. You've been in these woods a hundred times, but today, everything looks different. Tree leaves glow in golden sunlight. Wildflowers bloom all around as you and Sunny trot along the path. Rabbits hop out of hiding and birds swoop low, just to say hello.

Turn to page 38.

You and Sunny race through the woods until you reach an enormous tree. "I've never been here before!" you say.

"I have," says Sunny mysteriously. When she rubs her horn against the tree, you spot something shimmering on the bark. "Is that glitter?" you ask.

Sunny tosses her head. "It's fairy dust, silly!"

"Fairies?" you gasp.

"Of course," says Sunny, as if it's the most obvious thing in the world.

As the grass beside the tree starts to shake, you hold your breath. You have a feeling your "adventure" with your unicorn has only just begun . . .

The End

40

You tell Mason you're not ready to share your unicorn with the whole town. But as you ride Sunny away, you see the envy in Mason's eyes. He'd give *anything* to have a unicorn.

Later, when you go out back to say goodnight to Sunny, she's gone!

Mason, you think instantly. *Did he take her?* You race toward Grace's house and pound on the door.

Go on to the next page.

Grace says she hasn't seen Mason since dinner. "But he has a secret fort in the woods," she says, scooping her curls into a ponytail. "C'mon!"

Turn to the next page.

Grace flits through the yard so fast, you can barely keep up. You follow her through the shadowy woods until you reach a run-down cabin.

"Sunny?" you cry. You rush toward the cabin and find Mason—but no unicorn. "Where is she?"

Mason looks just as confused as you are. "I don't know what you're talking about," he says. "I came here looking for Waffles."

When he races back into the woods, you wonder if he's going in search of a missing dog—*or* a missing unicorn.

If you choose to look for clues at the cabin, turn to page 52.

If you choose to follow Mason, turn to page 62.

You loosen the reins and let Sunny turn around, away from the terrifying corn dog.

"Thank you, thank you, thank you," she says as she winds her way through the marching band.

Then you hear someone hollering, "Ben, look out!"

Sunny hears it, too. She whirls around. Ben is chasing after a butterfly—straight into the path of a clown car!

Go on to the next page.

Before you can tug on the reins to stop her, Sunny lunges toward Ben. You hang tight as Sunny scoops Ben into the air with her nose. Her witch hat topples sideways, and Ben flies through the air.

Turn to the next page.

Ben lands in the grass as the clown car zooms past. Then Sunny starts to tremble. "Goodness," she says. "That was close!"

"You did great," you say, even though your own heart is racing. "You saved Ben!"

Sunny shimmers. *Pop!* goes her horn—just as Mom and Mrs. Zimmerman race over.

You cross your fingers that Mom won't get upset about your unicorn. Sunny just proved that there's one thing she loves more than blueberries. She loves little kids like Jack and Ben.

When Mrs. Zimmerman throws her arms around Ben, Mom throws her arms around Sunny. "You saved the day!" Mom says. So maybe she'll let you keep your unicorn after all . . .

The End

Your parents agree to let you enter Sunny in the dog-and-pony act. They just don't know it's actually a dog-and-*unicorn* act.

The day of the show, you ride Sunny into the ring. With the smell of blueberry cotton candy in the air, she's never glowed so bright. *Pop!* Her horn sprouts. She trots so fast after Waffles, her hooves leave the ground. For a moment, you're actually flying!

You fling your arms around her neck. The audience gasps. And Mom's mouth drops open as you fly past. *Uh-oh.*

Turn to page 51.

When the judge hands you and your friends a blue ribbon, Mason pumps his fist. "I told you we'd win!" He doesn't seem to mind that your flying unicorn stole the show from his dog, Waffles.

Then Mom walks over, looking worried.

"Congratulations!" says the judge, pumping Mom's hand. "You must be so proud of your daughter and her unicorn!"

Mom's mouth twitches. "Um, y-yes," she stammers. "Of course."

Dad raves about Sunny all the way home. You and Sunny still have to win over Mom, but you're pretty sure you will. After all, what's not to love about a pet unicorn?

The End

You search the cabin, looking for any sign of your unicorn. Suddenly, you hear a sigh.

"Sunny?" you whisper. You've seen her coat fade when she's sad or scared. Could she have turned invisible?

"We need something that smells like berries," you say to Grace. "To make her happy again!"

Grace finds a tube of lip gloss in her sweatshirt pocket. "Will this work?" She unscrews the cap.

Go on to the next page.

"Blueberry?" you hear Sunny say. Before your eyes, her muzzle appears, and then her head and neck.

Turn to the next page.

Soon you see Sunny's shimmering body. You throw your arms around her. "Did Mason take you? I'm sorry, sweetie."

"No," she says. "Mason didn't take me. I came to find Waffles. But then it got so dark!"

"And you got scared?" asks Grace, patting Sunny's neck.

Sunny sighs.

You do, too. You might not be ready to share Sunny with the whole town. But she's definitely ready to get out of the stable. You won't be able to keep your unicorn a secret for much longer.

The End

You decide to tell your parents about Sunny tonight. But Sunny isn't ready to leave her buddy, Waffles. You practically have to drag her home. By the time you get there, it's raining. You hurry Jack through the front door and ride Sunny toward the stable.

As lightning flashes, Sunny starts to shake. "Oh, dear," she says. "Oh, dear!"

Then thunder rumbles. And Sunny bolts.

"Wait!" you cry, hanging on for dear life.

Sunny races past the stable. Through a neighbor's yard. And toward the trees in the distance.

You hear Mom call out behind you, but you can't stop!

Turn to page 58.

When Sunny reaches the trees, she finally stops. "S-sorry," she says, shivering.

"You don't like storms?" you ask Sunny.

Sunny hangs her head.

"The rain will clear up," you say gently. "Maybe we can play with Waffles again tomorrow!"

Sunny pricks her ears. She raises her head, and the rain slows down.

"I'll bet Dad's baking muffins right now," you say, trying to think of everything that makes Sunny happy.

"Blueberry?" she asks.

"Sure," you say. "Blueberry."

Go on to the next page.

Her coat glows so bright, you swear the sun just came back out. You glance up. The sun *did* come out! Did Sunny make that happen?

At the thought of blueberry muffins, Sunny pops her horn. She trots happily back toward home. But when you see Mom in the yard, you pull on the reins. "Wait!" you say. "Your horn!" Are you ready to show Mom your unicorn?

Poof! Sunny's horn disappears, and it starts to sprinkle.

"Are you okay?" cries Mom. She looks at Sunny as if she were a wild pony.

Sunny's head sinks. You hear her whisper sorry just as thunder rumbles overhead. Then she starts to shake. Is she going to bolt again?

Turn to page 61.

Just in time, Dad calls, "Breakfast for dinner? I made blueberry pancakes!"

Sunny starts to shimmer, and the clouds clear.

Mom shades her eyes against the sun. "What just happened?" she asks. She's so interested in the weather, she barely notices the unicorn in her yard.

Your stomach flutters. "I think my, um, unicorn can control the weather. Look, a double rainbow!"

"Fascinating!" says Mom. But she's looking at Sunny this time.

Mom says something about updating her weather software. "I predict this town will have a lot more sunny days from now on," she murmurs.

You think Mom's right!

The End

You hurry after Mason, who heads deeper into the shadowy woods. "Waffles!" he calls.

Grace skips to his side. "Is she really missing?" she asks, her voice rising.

He nods. "Waffles!"

Woof! A dog barks in the distance. You race forward but trip over a branch. It's *really* dark now.

Mason shines his flashlight and reaches down to help you up. "Are you okay?" he asks.

You suck in your breath. There, in the soft dirt, you see hoofprints. "Sunny's been here. Let's go!"

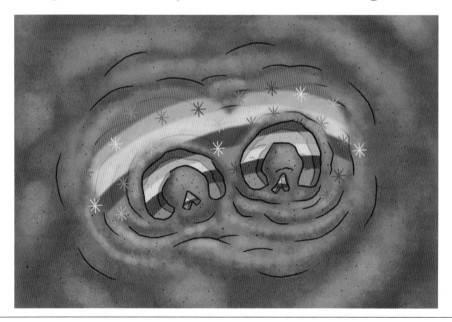

Go on to the next page.

You follow the hoofprints, which lead back to the cabin. Sunny is standing just outside the door!

"You were here all along!" you cry.

She hangs her head. "I came looking for Waffles," she says. "But it got so dark . . ."

Sunny's scared of the dark, you realize. "You can fix that," you remind her. "Just shine your horn!"

Sunny blinks. She scrunches her eyes shut, as if trying very hard. Then she sighs. "It's no use," she says.

Woof! A dog barks again in the distance.

And Sunny starts to glow.

Turn to the next page.

You ride Sunny back into the woods, her horn glowing like a lantern.

"Waffles!" cries Mason.

"Here, girl!" calls Grace.

As the barking grows louder, Sunny starts to trot.

Go on to the next page.

"Easy!" you cry as she dodges trees and leaps over logs. But there's no slowing her down.

Then a bush rustles near the path ahead.

Sunny stops so fast, you nearly fly off her back.

Turn to page 67.

Leaves shake, and a very dirty Waffles pops out of the bush. As Sunny leaps for joy, you slide off her rump.

"Waffles, naughty girl!" says Mason, pausing to catch his breath. "What are you doing out here?"

"Looking for me!" says Sunny. She closes her eyes happily as Waffles licks her muzzle.

"Best friends," says Grace, throwing her arm around your shoulders. "You just can't keep 'em apart."

You smile. "Nope." You're starting to see a dog-and-pony act in your future . . .

The End

ABOUT THE ARTIST

Darren McKee is a digital illustrator based in Texas with more than twenty years of experience. He has enjoyed a wide range of projects in advertising, publishing, and licensing. He specializes in children's books, editorial illustration, cartoonist, and character design. Clients include: Scholastic, Publications International, Scott Foresman, Lyrick Publishing, and Kimbery-Clark to name a few. When not working, he can be found in the great outdoors hiking with his wife, Debbie, in New Mexico and points west.

ABOUT THE AUTHOR

Erin Falligant loves writing multiple-ending books, because it's fun to imagine the many paths each story could take! She has written more than thirty books for children, including contemporary fiction, historical fiction, advice books, and picture books. Erin has a master's degree in child clinical psychology and worked as a children's book editor for more than fifteen years. To stay in touch with kids, she visits school classrooms and volunteers for the Madison Reading Project in her home state of Wisconsin.

For games, activities, and other fun stuff, or to write to Erin, visit us online at CYOA.com

Princess Peregrine Yvette

AKA Princess Perri

You can find me in:

Princess Island

Princess Perri and the Second Summer

Unicorn Princess

Age: 9

Favorite color: yellow

Likes: cooking, fixing stuff, the outdoors

Dislikes: fancy ball gowns and being a princess

HOMER

YOU CAN FIND ME IN:
SPACE PUP
LOST DOG!
HAUNTED HOUSE
RETURN TO HAUNTED HOUSE

AGE: in human or dog years?
FAVORITE FOOD: pizza
LIKES: time travel, french poodles, chewing shoes
DISLIKES: vacuums and the mail carrier